T0208614

No More Handcuffs

Alton Jamison

IUNIVERSE, INC.
NEW YORK   BLOOMINGTON

No More Handcuffs

iUniverse books may be ordered through booksellers or by contacting:

iUniverse
1663 Liberty Drive
Bloomington, IN 47403
www.iuniverse.com
1-800-Authors (1-800-288-4677)

Because of the dynamic nature of the Internet, any Web addresses or links contained in this book may have changed since publication and may no longer be valid.

ISBN: 978-1-4401-8929-6 (sc)
ISBN: 978-1-4401-8930-2 (ebk)

Printed in the United States of America

iUniverse rev. date: 11/30/2009

"The Choice"

For every positive thought in our head;
For every wish we might make.
For every good word we have said;
We limit our mistakes.

When we speak what we mean;
Our pride won't sink.
For the dreams that we all dream;
And the thoughts we all think.

Our reward will come in time;
The energy wasn't a waste.
In the end we will find;
A trophy for our good taste.

Let's not wait until the end;
To put our life in place.
If we choose to wait until then;
We still have GOD to face.

To keep us from being on the border;
GOD has shown us time.
We need to keep us all in order;
We just have to make up our mind.

Larry Alton Manley

HANDCUFFS:
AN INTRODUCTION

My name is Alton Jamison and I am many things. I am a Child of God. A Father. A Husband. A Son.

I am a Motivational Speaker. An Engineer. A Minister. A Successful Entrepreneur.

I am also an ex-convict.

I am other things as well. But, for our time together, I want to talk about my conviction.

The cops never arrested me. They didn't have to. I put the handcuffs on myself.

I took those cold steel loops, slipped them over my own wrists, and secured them. And, without even knowing it, I walked around in them for many years. You see, none of this happened in the physical realm. I was convicted in my mind.

Mentally, I locked myself away and served hard time. From the outside people couldn't see me sitting behind bars, on a cot, sporting the steel cuffs as if they were diamond-studded bracelets. From the outside people saw a young man struggling to pull himself up from nothing, a success-story in the making. They praised me and probably envied me, but last time I checked, no one envied jail. Had they known what was really going on—if they saw the real picture—they would have likely turned away.

I need you to know that if you're bound by similar chains you already have the tools to free yourself. If you're about to begin your own self-imposed sentence, know that your redemption is in hand.

I've chipped away at the wall, dug the tunnel, and filed the bars. I planned my escape and I want to show you the way out, too. Come with me. Don't be afraid. There's a better world beyond the prison gates. Let's just get these handcuffs off first. . .

PART I

A BRIDGE OVER TROUBLED WATERS

CHAPTER 1

I went to jail when I was nine years old.

I did not commit a crime, did not go before a judge, nor was I found guilty by a jury of my peers. When I went to jail, I went voluntarily.

It was the only way I could see my Dad.

Chesterfield County Sheriff's office was a fifteen minute drive from the house where I lived most of my life. To truly measure the distance though—what it meant in terms of its affect on my life and the lives of my family—required something more than the usual increments of minutes or miles.

It was springtime in Central Virginia and I wish I could say I remembered the trees in bloom, the warm breezes, and other beautiful signs of the season. But, none of those things were on my mind then and they're not in my memories now. What I remember is a slate gray block, a building surrounded by chain fences topped with razor wire and doors that looked strong enough to hold the Incredible Hulk. The fence was definitely designed to keep people locked in, both mentally and physically. I also remember the watch tower with the armed guards, ready to make a move at a moment's notice.

I rode in the back, my mom sat in the passenger seat and my grandfather drove. Visiting hours were every Saturday from 9am to 12pm. We approached the building by way of a concrete driveway leading to a guard shack adjacent to a locked gate. My grandfather braked, digging in his pocket for his wallet. A Deputy in his two-tone brown uniform and wide brim hat met us, and spoke like a robot set on auto-pilot. "IDs, please."

My grandfather handed over his driver's license and my mom passed over her ID. I didn't have an ID and I wondered if the guard would let me in. I was torn. At the start of the trip, I didn't want anything more than to see my Dad. Then, I saw where my Dad was, and half of me wanted the guard to turn me away. I secretly feared that if I entered that place, that jail, I would not be allowed to leave.

My eyes drifted then, from the cold dreariness of the jail house, to the black revolver propped on the guard's hip. I had a toy gun just like it . . . those were the days where no one thought twice about buying their young sons firearms or their young daughters babies. How many games of cops and robbers did I play with my toy? Like balls on a ping-pong table my eyes bounced from the guard's gun, back to the jailhouse.

How many games did my Dad play before toys and pretending lost their appeal?

"Who're you visiting today?" The Sheriff's Deputy asked, comparing the IDs to paperwork on his clipboard.

"My son," said my grandfather, "Manley. Larry Manley."

"And the boy?" The Deputy asked without looking my way.

"My grandson, Larry's son," he responded with a slight edge in his voice.

It felt like spring would become summer in the time it took the Deputy to check what he had to check and review whatever he had to review. From the clipboard, to the IDs, then finally to me, his gaze drifted. The Deputy passed back the IDs and patted the roof of the car the way a cowboy smacks a horse's rump to get it running. "Proceed through the gate, visiting hours are over at 12:00."

He retreated to his guard shack, pushed a button, and the gate before us slid open in a jerky motion while its motor whined and strained.

My grandfather shifted the car into gear and drove us into the heart of a place that will likely haunt me for the rest of my days.

*

They say in jury trials eye witness testimony is often quite fallible, contrary to popular belief. When a witness takes the stand and testifies that a defendant drove a red Chevrolet the night of an alleged crime, the defense might produce photographic evidence that the car in question was actually a Honda, and was in fact blue, and nowhere near the crime scene (trust me, this has happened before).

Now, what Hollywood would have you believe is when a witness is torn apart on the stand—found in total contradiction of actual events—the revelation leads to this avalanche of dramatic legal events. Music swells, the judge throws out the case, pounds his gavel triggering applause and praises to God from the defendant's family. All is well.

The truth: our legal system has been around for a long time. Not only are aspects of the law brought into court rooms, but aspects of psychology. The courts know full well that the human mind has trouble recalling detail, which is why few trials rely on a single eye witness.

The term is *corroboration*, more than one person confirms that the car was red, and was indeed a Chevrolet.

In my dad's case, there was plenty of corroboration. A lot of people saw him rob that bank.

He never bothered with the jury. He pleaded guilty, a smart move, considering the state had ample evidence to send him away until we were both old.

What could've been twenty years became five.

So, instead of playing catch football in the backyard on Saturday mornings, I spent time sitting on a steel bench bolted to the floor. Waiting.

Across the room a heavy steel door slid into the wall and two figures stood on the other side, bathed in harsh fluorescent light.

My mother nudged me, "Stand up for your father."

The man with my father, another Deputy, escorted my Dad over to us. It was a short distance; no more than ten yards, yet the process was painstakingly slow due to my Dad's condition. Shackles and handcuffs did not allow for expedient travel.

You know that thing about eye witnesses, how the human mind has trouble recalling detail? There are exceptions. In cases of extreme trauma, the mind can be branded with a memory that remains in vivid, startling clarity. That's how it was for me, then.

I loved my father, but seeing him in chains . . . it gouged me on the inside. If a Bengal Tiger had burst into the jailhouse and raked its six-inch claws across my chest, I doubt the scarring would be as deep as the image of my father *in bondage*. As the years passed I was able to conjure comparable images, things that helped me explain the pain of seeing him that way. But, explaining and conquering are two different things.

My dad shuffled over, his hair a little overgrown, but his beard trimmed neat. Despite his attire—the jailhouse orange jumpsuit didn't complement him one bit—he looked good. As good as could be expected anyhow.

"What's up, Champ?" He said, smiling with genuine joy.

"Hi," I chirped low.

It was around 9:30 by the time my Dad joined us. Two and a half hours of conversation passed, mostly between the adults at the table, and I'm sure I grew restless as any child would, though I cannot recall with certainty. What I do remember is the close of the conversation, the words that were just for he and I.

"You got your report card, didn't you? You did good, right." It wasn't a question.

"Yeah. I made honor roll. Only had one 'B'."

"In what?"

"Math."

He huffed, glanced around, "Yeah. That was always a tough one for me, too. You're smarter than me, though. You know that?"

I didn't know how to respond. It seemed like a mean thing to say you're smarter than someone, like teasing.

"You are," he answered for me.

I noticed a figure emerge in my periphery, the Sheriff's Deputy that brought my father in. "Time's up, Manley," he said, not unkindly.

My Dad's mouth tightened. He stood, but held my gaze. When he spoke again, his tone was different. Angry. "Look around. What do you think? Do you like it here?"

I froze for a second, teared up, unsure if he was mad at me. "No."

He held up his hands as far as the chain running from his ankles would allow, "You want a pair of these someday?"

I shook my head no, unable to answer verbally, my throat constricting to hold back sobs.

"Good," he said, his tone softening. He looked to the Deputy and nodded, and left without saying goodbye.

So, I said it for him, "bye."

He didn't look back as he walked into the guts of the jail, a place I could only imagine as horrible, cold, smelly and lonely.

He stepped into the corridor he'd emerged from, and before the heavy metal door separated me from him once again, he yelled out without looking back, "Don't end up like me." Then he was gone. With tears in my eyes, I said to myself, "I won't".

I had his eyes, his hair, his nose and his smile. If you let my Mom tell it, I had his attitude, too. "Don't end up like me," he said. Even at that age, I had to wonder . . . <u>did I have a choice?</u>

*

Throughout the book, I will ask you several questions that I want you to first reflect on and then write down your answers. Don't rush through the questions, but take your time with each one and allow your mind to process each answer carefully. The first set of questions are below:

Questions
1) Has a family member, loved one or close friend in your life ever made a bad decision? How did you know it was bad?
2) How did their bad decision make you feel about them? About yourself?
3) Have their bad decisions affected your own decision making? How?

CHAPTER 2

I grew up in a small city. Hopewell, Virginia. Population 23,000. Home of the Blue Devils.

It was a town born of industry, the base for chemical plants exhaling fat clouds from smokestacks overlooking the Appomattox River, a beautiful body of water . . . if you didn't look too close. More famous for the musty stench emanating from the industrial yards than much of anything else, naming the town "*Hope*well" sometimes seemed like sarcasm on the part of the founders.

But, it was home. Not always positive and encouraging, but home all the same. And I learned to make the best of it anyway I could. I realized early on that even with my Dad locked away I still had two up on most of my peers. One, at least I knew who my Dad was. Two, I did have a father figure in-house.

I have no memory of my mother and father being together romantically. They remained friendly, and she showed compassion for his unfortunate incarceration, of course. Otherwise, I've never seen the current of love pass between my parents other than through the obvious conduit. Me.

My mother's heart belonged to a kind-hearted and quiet man with an affinity for cold beer. His name was Jesse Brown, my mother's love and my stepfather. He stood in while my biological father was out of the picture, and for that, I am eternally grateful.

But, that's not to say I was always happy with my home life.

I can't say we were poor, because I can never recall a time where I'd gone hungry, but poor was how I felt on more days than I cared to remember. My mother made just above minimum wage as a fast-food worker and my stepfather did a bit better as a private parcel courier. We (my mother, stepfather, and two sisters) shared a 900 square-foot house deeded to my stepfather from his grandmother, and on too many nights I can recall the staccato tapping of rain water dripping into strategically placed pots and pails.

It was on those nights that I had what I liked to call The Huxtable Fantasy, named after the iconic African-American family spawned from Bill Cosby's imagination.

In the Huxtable Fantasy, my house wasn't on a tilted foundation with a leaky roof. It was a three-level Brooklyn brownstone, bright and warm. My mom was a successful business woman who wore suits and makeup to work. And my dad . . . was there. Not locked in a cell, but free and living up to the potential he'd forsaken long ago. Maybe not a doctor like Heathcliff Huxtable, but something other than behind bars.

I spent a lot of time upset with all of the adults in my life. My dad for not being there, and my mom and stepfather for the lifestyle in which I felt imprisoned. What I couldn't see then was the strength it took for all of them to maintain what I so eagerly dismissed as meager.

How easy was it to be locked away from your family for years?

How easy was it to raise another person's child?

How easy was it to get up every day and trudge to a thankless, low-paying job to feed your household?

I couldn't understand those things then. And, in those formative years I had a festering anger, one that if left unchecked by the likes of my mother and stepfather, would've likely found me on the same path my father walked, a path like the peers with whom I spent many of my days.

*

In the 80's, Hopewell, Virginia was far from the gang-infested streets of Chicago or the drug trafficking of Miami. It wasn't even as bad as its neighbor to the north, Richmond, the state's capital. In most regards my hometown was docile in terms of crime, a safe place for children to play until the street lights came on. Therein lied the danger, not in the streets, but in the damaged children becoming damaged adults before their time. Learning manhood through assumptions instead of actual men.

A nuclear family (mother, father, kids), living together under one roof was the exception, not the norm. As a result, a generation of angry sons grew and congregated; and their aggression was acted out on playgrounds, basketball courts and football fields.

I found my release honing athletic skills to best the next young man. The same way others felt shame in not knowing their father, I was embarrassed about my Dad's status as a resident of the state. Every Saturday morning, for the years between my ninth and fourteenth birthday, I'd take a ride to Chesterfield county jail, sit with my old man for a few hours, and be back in time to join a pickup basketball game in the early afternoon.

To the best of my friend's knowledge, I just liked to sleep late.

I never had to explain my absence during those visits the same way another boy didn't have to explain that his mom had a new boyfriend with no qualms about stern hand-to-hand discipline when he'd show up to the playing field with a fresh black eye. We all knew each other's situation, and all avoided conversation about it. In that avoidance a touch football game might become unexpectedly brutal, or a fist fight might break out over the high score on *Super Mario Bros.* Our alternate expressions of root pain became as varied as the crossword puzzles in the daily paper.

Except at home, for me anyway.

I could cut up with my friends, play dirty, curse or whatever. But, when I got home, certain behavior was not tolerated. Even after a long day at grueling jobs, my Mother and Stepfather had no trouble finding energy to keep me in check. Too many of my friends didn't have that. And, the differences started to show. Many of my friends that I grew up with started hanging on the corners with the crowd known for selling drugs and getting into other types of trouble. Every day I would see some of my close friends going from the school bus to the corner instead of going home. Part of me wanted to be with them, because they were my friends, but the other part of me wanted to go home out of respect for my mom. Whenever I saw my friends, the words of my father echoed in my head, "don't end up like me".

*

I found academics as stimulating as sports, more so since I was never an all-star athlete. There was pleasure in besting my classmates with a solid report card the same way there was in hitting a game winning jump-shot in a basketball game. Some of my friends began to find their pleasures on the street corners, with older boys learning a different type of game than the ones we grew up playing together. Others found their pleasures in the opposite sex.

In all of my peers, I saw my father's life, two-fold. Some went to jail, some had kids. The overachievers did both. They became parents when they couldn't even fathom the responsibility any more than their newborn could fathom calculus. Then, almost as if the two acts came as a package, they might completely throw away their youth by getting locked up over some silly drug or weapons charge. As more of them fell victim to the trappings of a life disregarded, my father's words echoed in my skull.

Don't end up like me.

No problem. That part was common sense. But, the strange thing about being a young teen is what earns you the respect of your peers often goes against common sense. While doing the right thing—the <u>smart</u> thing—results in shunning akin to lepers in the Bible.

I got good grades, so I was a 'nerd'. I used proper grammar and syntax when I spoke, so 'I thought I was white'. I socialized with people of other races, so 'I thought I was better than my own people'. Thank goodness for athletics. Because I could run fast and, at 5'6", did not show fear when facing someone 6'5" on the line of scrimmage, I got a slight reprieve. When my peers said those mean things about me, they might laugh afterwards and slap me on the back so I'd know it was all in good fun. Right?

The summer after my fourteenth birthday I prepared to enter Hopewell High School as a freshman. A four-year countdown to a better life and better opportunities began. Summer meant football practice, two-a-days. And, that was really all my mind was on.

One morning, after I chomped down some Frosted Flakes and got my head together for the day's grueling drills in 100 degree heat, I stepped on my porch just as the exterior door opened and a man stepped in.

My stomach lurched.

"You look like you seen a ghost," he said.

"Dad?"

There he was. No orange jumpsuit, no chains. I'd barely recognized him without them.

"That's right, son. I'm home now."

I gave him a hug and in my mind I thought a guard was going to come tap him on the shoulder telling him that time is up for today. I can't believe that my dad is finally home. We can finally be a family again.

Questions
1) Have you always run with a crowd, or do you do your own thing? Either way, how do people treat you for your choice?
2) When situations get you down, how do you cope?
3) Do you think your coping mechanisms yield good results or bad ones?

CHAPTER 3

When I was in high school I sang in the Glee Club.

At Hopewell High it wasn't called Glee Club, mind you. We we're *Mixed Company* — our title and definition. A show choir of 8 boys and 8 girls who performed at churches, banquets, nursing homes, in competitions, and at school assemblies.

For many reasons, the times we performed on our school's stage were my least favorite.

I was fifteen when I joined Mixed Company, a sophomore with one year down and three to go before I'd be released from a prison I didn't even know I was in. My grades were still good, my diction still proper, so the level of ridicule I'd experienced through most of my youth had not diminished.

Singing sappy songs in a Teddy Bear sweater and a Santa hat at Christmas did not help my plight one bit.

So, why do it? Simple: my Dad wouldn't have.

He'd been home for over a year, given a new lease on life so to speak. Here was an opportunity for the former honor student and All-State Wrestler to find the path he'd been destined to travel before he turned to crime. The bank robbery was behind him, his debt to society paid. Those handcuffs and shackles that hindered his progress for all those Saturdays were gone.

Physically, anyway.

It's no secret that it's hard for felons to find gainful employment once released from prison. If they did not have a valued trade, such as barbering or mechanical skills, it could be downright impossible to make ends meet. In that regard, my father was resourceful. Always a good cook, he had no problem finding work in local diners and clubs. To say he excelled at the culinary arts would not have been an understatement.

In my mind, I saw infinite possibilities for him. A good cook could become a great chef. A great chef could open a fabulous restaurant. A fabulous restaurant could become a culinary empire.

I only wish his thoughts mirrored mine.

Where I saw roads, he saw roadblocks.

When I mentioned my ideas to him the resulting conversation would come off like a debate, pros and cons.

"Dad, you could go to culinary school," I might say.

"I can't pay for that type of thing. Hard enough to make rent."

He still carried the mentality one had to have when living in a cell. Watch your back, trust no one. If it seemed like a good thing, it was probably a setup and should be avoided at all costs. The jail let him go, but mentally he was still incarcerated.

But, that original piece of advice he gave me still rang true. <u>Don't end up like me.</u>

In him, I found an arch role model. If he did it, I did the opposite. If he said something seemed too hard, I sought it out. When he dated numerous women, I committed fully and completely to my high school sweetheart. Oddly, in that dichotomy we grew closer, magnets drawn together by the strength of our opposing force.

Now, I wonder if my Dad was more clever than I gave him credit for. Perhaps he noticed the spark of defiance in me, and used it to push me as far away from the path he traveled as possible.

Maybe that's why he stayed on that road to destruction . . . to save me. I tried hard to figure out an angle, a noble cause to discern how a genuinely good man could make bad decisions over and over again.

When I was 18, I graduated from Hopewell High as the class President with a GPA that ranked in the top 15% of my class. My dad came, took pictures with me, and for once did not play ying to my yang. He told me he was proud of me and we were on the same page for one of the few times in my life. I was proud of him just for making it, not only to my graduation, but to that point in his life, after all he'd been through.

There was no way to tell, on that joyous night, that my dad was harboring a secret and, in less than 10 years, I'd be standing over his coffin wondering, *what happened?*

Questions
1) Is there someone in your life whom you'd like to model yourself after? Why?
2) Is there someone in your life whom you absolutely, positively DON'T want to model yourself after? Why?
3) Name two people whose actions surprised you in a good way and in a bad way?

CHAPTER 4

After high school, I attended college at Old Dominion University. I majored in Mechanical Engineering and minored in having fun. College life was a great experience. In college, I had an opportunity to network and meet people from a variety of backgrounds. I was fortunate enough to meet my wife while I was in college, which further proves my point.

Throughout my college career, I kept in contact with my father. We would talk occasionally over the phone and see one another in person a couple of times of year. Even after I graduated and was married, we stayed in contact periodically. He would talk about how proud he was of me and I would try to encourage him to go back to school or try to do something different to secure his own future.

The last time I spoke to my father was his birthday, February 16th, 2004. Sadly, it wasn't a pleasant conversation. He'd called my wife earlier that day asking for 1,800 dollars because he was behind on his rent. It wasn't the first time he'd turned to me for financial relief, and to be honest, I was frustrated by it.

When my wife gave me the message, I called him back, more than a little irritated, "Dad, I'm sorry. I can't do it this time. I've got bills and a household to support and 1800 dollars is a lot of money. And really I don't think it's right that you always turn to me for financial support. You're a grown man."

There comes a point when everyone falls on some sort of hard times, and I didn't intend to kick him when he was down, but what I said was true. And, it didn't help that I felt justified. He hadn't been around for so much of my life, doing the things he was supposed to do to raise me. Now, I'm supposed to support him? He couldn't-and shouldn't-expect me to pull him out of the fire all the time.

Needless to say, the conversation didn't go well.

When I hung up the phone on that Monday. I was ticked off, and I knew I wouldn't hear from my Dad for awhile, because he was ticked off too. So what?

I shrugged it off and went about my normal routine. After all, that's what I'd done my entire life. He zipped in and out of my world like a fly at a barbeque, buzzing onto unguarded plates taking what it could get and returning when it could get more. That was just one of the many evil, disrespectful thoughts I conjured during the week following that conversation. Even with the ugliness in my head, I felt the urge to call him back and I didn't know why.

I fought that urge though. Pride reigned supreme over me.

I couldn't figure what good would come of it and frankly, I didn't feel like dealing with any of his nonsense. Not then.

But I had to deal with my father much sooner than I expected when the police fished his corpse out of the James River.

Questions
1) Has someone ever hurt you to the point that you felt like you couldn't go on? How did you make it through?
2) Have you ever hurt someone and regretted it? Were you able to make amends?
3) Is there anything in your life that you feel guilty about but you're afraid you can never resolve the issue?

CHAPTER 5

Four days after that conversation with my father, my uncle called me and asked if I was sitting down. He said that my dad had committed suicide by jumping from the Lee Bridge in Richmond, Va. I momentarily felt that my life was paused and I begin to have flashbacks about my life and my father's life. Saying to myself, "what if I had given him the money?" In my disbelief, I rushed home to be with my family.

Tears rolled down my eyes as I sat in my grandfather's house and watched the six o'clock news. To most of the people across Central Virginia, the unidentified man SCUBA divers dragged out of the James River was just another morbid report. To them, it probably wasn't the worst story of that day, not when you factored in the war in Iraq or the latest silly scandal out of Hollywood. To them, the waterlogged face was one they wouldn't recognize anyway. The life that cold river water extinguished was one that had no effect whatsoever on their world.

*

This part sounds like a lie. It sounds like the stuff of good (or bad) melodramas. It's the type of emotional reaction I would've called 'corny' in earlier times.

But times do change.

My Dad leapt off the Lee Bridge in Richmond, Virginia and fell 300 feet to an icy death. I wanted to know what that was like.

For most of my life I'd dedicated myself to being the exact opposite of the man who brought me into this world. But, on a cloudy day, with mid-day traffic whizzing by behind me, I wanted to be just like him. I wanted to know what he thought when he walked to the guardrail. I wanted to know what the water looked like when it wasn't just a pretty view, but a gateway into eternity.

That next day, I went to the Lee Bridge in Richmond, Va. I stepped onto the sidewalk with the sound of cars passing in the background. You could still see the black finger print dust left on the guardrails. I placed my hands on the top rail and my left foot on the bottom rail.

I could just imagine drivers and passengers zooming across the bridge, watching me. Maybe some of them dialed 911 on their cell phones to warn the police of a jumper. Perhaps some of them paid me no mind because I wasn't a part of their world. I glanced back at that traffic, then forward at the open air over the water. The current along the shoreline was choppy, devouring the jagged river rocks before receding back into itself. It seemed unorganized, as if nature's plan had gone awry and the river was unsure of what to do and how to do it.

Troubled water.

I leaned over, then looked into the distance. I said quietly to myself, "I won't end up like you…I won't."

I lowered myself back onto the concrete walkway. My father was gone.

Not in jail. Not angry and emotionally despondent. Gone.

As always, those five words came back. <u>Don't end up like me.</u> It was like this final act was his exclamation point on the statement.

That couldn't be it, though. It couldn't be. Don't end up like me wasn't good enough. Because the statement said, "My life is done. Try not to let yours end this way." That wasn't the case, not at all, but my Dad believed it, so for him it was true. It was like he'd thrown himself off the bridge 20 years ago, and the world was just catching up with him.

The last time we'd spoken was probably the worst sort of conversation we could've had, given the circumstances. But, I can say that my guilt was minimal. I'd honored his ultimate wish . . . I wasn't like him. And I know without a doubt that my end will not be the same as his.

But there, on that bridge that day, it wasn't good enough.

What good was saving myself if I couldn't save anyone else?

That's where my guilt sprang from, my inability to truly help my father. He'd left the jailhouse a decade prior, but he'd never taken off the handcuffs. And, in that sense, I was like him.

We were fugitives on the run, two separate personalities, two separate objectives, forced to stick together because of the cuffs on our wrists. Now, he was dead, and the cuffs were still there. On me.

It chained me to him and chained me to my selfish beliefs. My whole life had been a self-centered pursuit to be better than him, to spite him in the name of honoring him. I dragged him through my successes the same way he dragged me through his failures . . . by the cuffs on our wrists.

Now that he was gone, I had a choice. I could leave the cuffs on, dragging his corpse around, bitter and angry over his inability to move how I moved. Or, I could free myself and let him rest. I could move swiftly and really honor his memory by not only making sure I didn't end up like him, but making sure others didn't either.

All I had to do was take off the cuffs.

My gaze drifted back to the river, and I had another vision, much clearer than the dreary images of the night my father died. I pictured myself tossing off those cuffs, flinging them into the water. And, I pictured my dad on the horizon, smiling, enjoying the fact that one of us was finally going to get it right.

I walked back to my car, leaving the Lee Bridge behind, but not really. From that point forward, I've thought about that structure quite often. Because on that day, me and The Lee Bridge gained a very distinct commonality.

Just like it, I became a bridge over troubled water.

Questions:
1) Have you ever had a moment of clarity that let you know maybe you weren't doing things the way you're supposed to? What was it?
2) Can you think of 2 to 3 defining moments in your life that let you know you are here for a bigger purpose?
3) What area of your life do you still have handcuffs on?

Part II

Five Keys to the Handcuffs

THE FIRST KEY:
THE PAST DOES NOT
DETERMINE THE FUTURE

Back to the Future, that old sci-fi comedy starring Michael J. Fox, is one of my favorite films.

Not only is it well-written and well-acted, the idea of a young man going back in time to change the history of his family intrigued me in ways I could never rationalize until recently.

If there were such a thing as a time-traveling De Lorean, then there's no question *when* my first temporal destination would be. I'd go back to my father's childhood and make sure he understood the great potential living within him. But, the ability to change the past is pure fantasy and there's no need to dwell in the world of make-believe.

Especially when the power to alter the future is as real as this book you now hold in your hands.

Clichés and catch phrases propagate ideas that our destinies are out of our hands. Either directly or indirectly they tell us that the way we are born is the way we're going to live and eventually die . . . good, bad or indifferent.

The apple doesn't fall far from the tree.
You can't teach an old dog new tricks.
Like father, like son.

First off, let me say this as plainly and as clearly as possible. None of these idioms *has* to be true *if you don't want them to be true.*

Don't misunderstand, there are many of you out there who undoubtedly want to be very much like your parents, or continue to maintain lifestyles and attitudes that you've known since birth. There's nothing wrong with that whatsoever, if that's your choosing. But know you are not *bound* by anything that has come before you.

You don't need to take my words as proof (though I think the evidence here is solid). We all see this principle in action every day, positively and negatively.

Look at the current crop of celebrity youth who are *born* into the lap of prestige and influence. Many of these young adults are given every opportunity in the world to be a light for others, as many of their parents have been. Yet, we most often hear of their drunken escapades or stints in jail.

On the flip-side of the coin an abused child does not have to become an adult who abuses children.

A child who is shuttled in and out of foster care does not have to be an adult who creates a series of broken homes.

But, you have to believe that . . . because others won't.

In *Back To The Future*, Michael J. Fox's character, Marty McFly, is told early in the film by his high school principal Mr. Strickland, "You're a slacker, you've always been a slacker, just like your old man. No McFly ever amounted to anything."

I hope and pray that you do not have a Mr. Strickland in your life essentially telling you you're worthless and prophesying failure into your life when he has no more knowledge of the future than a stone in the road. But, if there is a person like that in your life, you have to understand they are there for a reason.

They're there to help you decide if you're really a failure or not.

Nothing I've ever done has been easy.

Everything I've ever done that's worth doing has made me want to quit.

Now, take a moment to absorb those two statements.

After I finished college, I decided that I didn't want to be one of the people who spent their whole life working for a company only to retire and then be forced to get a part-time job because their pension isn't paying their monthly bills. In my view, a J.O.B. stands for "Just Over Broke" and I didn't want to live like that. This was around the time in the early part of this millennium when the real estate market was on fire.

I got a great deal on a little three-bedroom, one-bath brick rancher in my home town. The house belonged to my grandfather who was tired of the real estate game, but more than willing to give me my start. There was a tenant in the place at the time of purchase, so going into it I had an additional stream of income. I thought, *it's really this easy?*

It really wasn't.

Shortly after I took ownership, the tenant's lease expired and they decided to move on. They vacated the property, and I decided to check the place out before putting up a for rent sign for new tenants.

I don't think I've seen a horror movie as scary as what I experienced when I stepped through the door of that house.

I flipped the light switch and fluorescent bulbs flared bright, spotting my vision. At least I thought they were spots.

Dots scattered across my line of sight. Dots with legs and antennae. The sudden rush of moment gave me a sense of vertigo, my mind could not process all the information at once.

Literally HUNDREDS of roaches infested the house, so great in number, that my presence only startled them momentarily. With the house vacant and no furniture to offer cover, the vermin did not bother hiding. Why should they? I was on their turf.

Every surface seemed to gyrate, as if the walls and floor were living, rippling things. The activity in the house reminded me of a child's Ant Farm, a colony hard at work.

Bile rose like lava in the back of my throat. I was so disgusted by the sight of the creatures that my skin tingled for hours afterward. I imagined the little creatures under my suit jacket, inside the collar of my shirt, scurrying up my sleeves, into my armpits and underwear. Then, I realized I wasn't imagining.

I'd backed into a wall, and a few of the creatures had gotten on me.

I burst out of the house as if it was on fire. I stood in the front yard, flung my jacket to the ground, and just about stripped naked in broad daylight. Before I started to peel off my garments, I realized I had flung the roaches off me already. Good thing, too . . . I don't think the neighbors were in the mood for a strip show.

When I calmed down, I sat in my car, staring at the house, and wondering, what have I gotten myself into?

The next time I returned to my house, I came with an exterminator. He pulled on a jumpsuit and equipment that reminded me of *Ghostbusters* and went about inspecting the house. I was not surprised when he emerged twenty minutes later and announced, "The infestation in this house is one of the worst I've ever seen."

So, I wrote him a check and kissed a significant chunk of the profits I'd accumulated from the house goodbye.

The pest problem was the first of many. Structural, plumbing, roof and cooling problems were quickly added to the list, and before long, I was no longer paying for services out of the profits I'd accumulated. I was paying out of my own pocket.

This whole landlord business wasn't fun, wasn't profitable, and was just an overall pain in the you-know-what.

And, on top of that, inside my head I could hear the voices of a few of my friends who balked at my idea of becoming a real estate investor.

That's a lot of work, they said.

What if the tenants don't pay their rent, they said.

All I could think about was how right they were. It was a lot of work, and I wasn't liking the responsibility of fixing up a place only to have another tenant come in and possibly trash it all over again.

Then came that point.

You know which one I'm talking about. It was the point where I could see two distinct possibilities—two distinct risks—and, in that moment, I could decide the future.

A) I could cut and run. I could sell the house, take a minor loss and give up on real estate or B)I could tough it out and possibly deal with more ridiculous housing situations.

Option A had the lowest risk because it contained the risk I'd already taken. I'd stepped out, didn't like what I saw, and I could reverse my decision. By reversing the decision, I'd determine the future through negative reinforcement. The situation would be equivalent to gambling, losing the bet, and being wise enough not to make the bet again. If I sold the property, I'd no longer have to worry about the upkeep of that literal ROACH MOTEL, but I'd also never become a real estate mogul because I'd gotten burned. I'd have to find another entrepreneurial avenue . . . if I even wanted to be an entrepreneur at all anymore.

Without a doubt, if my past did indeed determine my future option A was the option I'd *have* to take.

What I'd seen and lived most of my life was an attitude of submission. If it's hard or risky, don't do it, just take what life decides to give you. You may not always like the hand you're dealt, but at least you could blame the dealer for it.

Option B had the highest risk because it represented the risk I'd yet to take. I could continue on with the house renovations, sinking more money into what could be a deep, sucking money pit. I could possibly get a tenant in there willing to pay the rent that would cover the mortgage. And, if that worked out for a few months, I could try to purchase another potential money pit. There were a million ways this real estate nonsense could go wrong.

How many times have you been faced with a choice like that? How many times did you take the easy way out? There's no shame in that, understand. Not every risk is meant to be taken. But, how many of those passed-over risks do you look back on now and wonder what your life would have been like today had you stuck with them?

How many times have you realized you could've changed your future?

During the period when I could've given up on real estate, all of those thoughts crossed my mind, and, albeit reluctantly, I stuck in there, and did the hard thing. Not only did I do the hard thing, but I made it harder by buying my next house less than two months after finishing the renovations on my first house.

Today, I can say with pride that I now have a small real estate empire. I won't say a dollar amount because that tends to stand out more than the message, but I can honestly say that it was one of the best decisions I ever made, despite the hard times. By taking that opportunity to change my future, in spite of my past, I now have the freedom to enjoy life on a level most people only fantasize about.

Questions
1) What are some easy choices you made that you now regret?
2) What will you do the next time you have a choice between easy and hard?
3) Do you allow things in your past to determine your future?

THE SECOND KEY:
USE PRESSURE TO BUILD MUSCLE

Do you know much about deep sea life?

If you don't, that's fine, I have some information I hope you find interesting. If you do, bear with me to see how much you have in common with the New Zealand Fangtooth Fish.

*

We've all heard that the earth is more than 75% water. It's funny because though the majority of our planet is made up of water, we know relatively little about it. We know we need it to survive, that it makes up most of our bodies, but in terms of its depths and what lives there beneath our oceans, our body of knowledge is small.

We know more about outer space than we know about the water all around us. After all, we've walked on the moon, but have yet to walk in the deepest trenches of the oceans.

Why? We can't handle the pressure.

For us humans, sinking too deeply without the protection of a pressurized submersible would be the same as stepping into a hydraulic car crusher. Yet, even at the greatest depths, under the most extreme pressure, life thrives.

By no means am I qualified to discuss the ins and outs of oceanography or marine biology, but I do recognize a parallel between the lives of creatures like the New Zealand Fangtooth and the human ability to thrive under pressure.

As I've told you, I studied engineering in college. The classes I took and the principles I learned were mind numbing at times, but in 2001 I received my diploma on a Sunday. There was scarce time to celebrate because on Monday I started my full-time job as an associate engineer at Newport News Shipbuilding in Newport News, Virginia.

I'd interned at the shipyard for 3 years prior to becoming a full-time employee so my experience there had always been coupled with grueling class schedules, late-night cram sessions, and trying to maintain some semblance of a real-life. In other words, the hardest thing in my life (school) made everything else seem hard by proxy.

But, school was behind me. And I found my assignments as an associate engineer differed very little from my work as an intern. I was making a decent wage, I purchased my first home at a good price, and had no real obligations outside of showing up at the office eight hours a day.

All of a sudden, life was easy.

And, secretly, I hated it.

After struggling for so long, after scrambling to get everything, I'd 'arrived' . . . but I didn't know if I liked the destination.

Easy things become monotonous. It wasn't long before my good paying job became a grind. Five years of schooling and I spent most of my day typing different numbers in the same Excel spreadsheets over and over. One of those free classes at the public library could've prepared me for that.

Finally, I found myself using computers and calculators to figure equations I used to be able to do by hand (as everyone in my office did). The rationale was computers don't make mistakes, people do. But, in a brief moment of revelation, I realized I *had* to rely on the computer to get it right because I couldn't remember how to do the equation on my own (though I'd done hundreds of similar equations during my time in grade school and college). My mind—the muscle I'd spent years of time and thousands of dollars to build up—had atrophied. There was a direct correlation between the weakening of my 'mind-muscle' and my growing dissatisfaction with my oh-so-easy daily routine.

Do you know what happens to the New Zealand Fangtooth if you capture it and drag it to the surface?

It explodes.

Perhaps not literally, but in essence, after spending it's whole life existing under the crushing pressure at the ocean floor, its body cannot cope without that pressure. When there's no crushing force surrounding it, its internal systems expand, still pushing against a force that's no longer there.

In a no-pressure situation, the New Zealand Fangtooth does not thrive, it dies.

The way I see it, most people are either just like the New Zealand Fangtooth or the complete opposite. Either one can be worked with.

If you're at the top of whatever it is you do—you're the fittest, the smartest, the richest—you've likely lived and thrived under great pressure already. Good for you.

Now, don't let up.

The time you've spent struggling to get where you are has developed a strength within you. Your resolve is like tensile steel. Don't lose it. You need to maintain the level of pressure you experienced to get where you are . . . and, in some cases, you may need to crank it up a notch.

My real estate business has garnered me a small fortune. As you know, it had a tough beginning and there have been tough times since, but my company functions and functions well. I could sit back, let my properties appreciate, and get rich from very little effort.

That sort of complacency just doesn't work for me. In my mind, if I took that route, it would not be long before I started slacking on my duties within my company. After all, if a task is cake, then it doesn't need to be watched. You put cakes in the oven and walk away. In order for me to stay sharp, I need more pressure.

All have the potential, mind you, but everyone cannot handle the same degrees of pressure. And, I can all but guarantee you that the wilder the dream, the greater the pressure you'll have to thrive in to accomplish it.

There are exceptions. If you won the Mega-Millions lottery tomorrow then you would've eliminated the number one deterrent of dream pursuit for most people: money. To most of you, this sounds great. Sudden financial stability can't be a bad thing, right? Well, maybe.

Say you always wanted to be a florist. You had dreams of owning your own small-town flower shop, designing arrangements for weddings, making sure couples stayed in love on Valentine's Day, and so on. But, you hadn't drawn up a true business plan, never put start-up money aside. In other words, you never stepped out of the dream realm and dealt with the reality of what it takes to run a business.

Then—*BAM!!*—the next day you hit the lottery. More money than you ever imagined is sitting in your bank account ready to be spent. All of sudden, it's easy to start your flower shop. Business plan? What business plan? Banks and investors are the ones who want to see business plans, and you don't need any of them. They use business plans to decide if a venture is a risk or not, but with millions at your disposal there is no risk.

You open your shop feeling no pressure at all.

Business goes smoothly at first. You're calling the shots, you're pocketing the profits . . . only, and there are no profits. You haven't had the first customer. You're bored and frustrated, and that teenage kid you hired called in sick with the Ebola virus (though he seems well enough to skateboard in the parking lot outside your shop). There's a stack of city, state and federal paperwork on your desk that needed your attention yesterday and the flowers are dying.

All of a sudden you go from no-pressure to swimming right alongside the New Zealand Fangtooth.

To maintain the business, you have to thrive in the pressure, but because you did not gain a gradual resistance and the accompanying strength to maintain in such conditions, it becomes that much harder to survive. I cannot say with certainty what a person would do at this point, but it's been my experience that a person who has never had to survive such pressure will seek less pressure, not more.

In the case of the flower shop, you bail.

That's a grim example, discouraging even. I know. But I need you to understand you can't just make a jump from no pressure, to heavy pressure. If you're not used to a pressure-filled life, you need to increase your pressure gradually, build the strength to thrive in that pressure, and above all, know your limits.

Everyone has a dream, a dream that seems impossible. I can't tell you it's not impossible. But, that's the point, if anyone can tell you your dream is unachievable, and you believe them . . . well, need I say more?

If you're the type of person who doesn't care what others say, but have a hard time fathoming how you can become the CEO of your own company, or write your first novel, or become a stand-up comedian when you've never done anything of the sort, then I have a fairly simple solution to get you started.

Turn up the pressure so you can build the strength to thrive. Obviously, it can take years to accomplish your ultimate goal, but by turning up the pressure just a little, you can get going in the right direction. If you want to run a company, start working towards a management position in whatever vocation you're currently in. Even if you're working at your local burger stand, find out how a burger stand works. Learn how the money is spent, how the supplies are ordered, how schedules are made.

And, more importantly, find a mentor who can tell you what to expect when the pressure increases. You can't swim with a Fangtooth if you don't know a Fangtooth.

Questions
1) What is something that you've always wanted to do but have not done? What's stopping you?
2) How can you gradually turn up the pressure to achieve that goal?
3) Name 3 people that would be good mentors to help you get to the next level in your life.

THE THIRD KEY: STEREOTYPES SHOULD MOTIVATE YOU, NOT DEFINE YOU

African-Americans are lazy.
Caucasians are racist.
Jews are greedy.
And so on.

I don't know if you've heard any of those foolish and reprehensible statements before, but I have, unfortunately. And they don't stop there. Stereotypes are as varied and ugly as the monsters in all the children's fairy tales combined . . . and they're just as imaginary. There is no one statement that covers every single person in any specific group, yet, how many hundreds of millions of people believe that to be the case? And, worse, how many of you believe such silly things about whatever group you belong to?

Several years ago, I volunteered as a mentor/facilitator for a group called, Operation Understanding Hampton Roads. The group was a year-long diversity program targeted at bridging the gap between African American and Jews. The composite of the group were African American and Jewish 10th and 11th graders from the surrounding areas. These students were all from the top of their class and had to make it through a highly selective application process.

The program involved taking the students on civil rights tours, visiting holocaust museums and meeting survivors and many more amazing events to bring a sense of meaning to the program. Through this program, I learned several keys:

1) Stereotypes can only be true if you give into the stereotype.
2) Prejudice is hatred by insecure people, your job is to remain secure in yourself and don't succumb to their level.
3) You have to change you before you can change anybody else.

Let's examine the first key, "Stereotypes can only be true if you give into the stereotype." Stereotypes, regardless of race and ethnic backgrounds are a tinted view and certain people's way of defining a population. I can use myself as an African American male. If I allow a stereotype of being lazy or fathering numerous children out of wedlock to define me, then that is who I will become. Even though none of these characteristics fit me, I can become a victim of giving into what society thinks of me. No more handcuffs means that you don't allow popular opinion to place boundaries and strongholds on you and definitely not your destiny. In my mind, I define my own stereotypes. For example, anyone that reads this book will be on track for a successful life. Or anyone that chooses to remove their "mental handcuffs" will open the door to many unseen opportunities. You must define you, not let the news media, BET, MTV or ESPN do it for you.

The second key is, "Prejudice is hatred by insecure people, your job is to remain secure in yourself and don't succumb to their level." Prejudice has held people in bondage for much too long. Quite often, people holding these prejudices are insecure in themselves. You are a leader. You are destined for something greater and you cannot allow a prejudice to hold you back. Prejudices are not always "black" and "white". It could be prejudices about people's weight, the school they went to or even their last name. Regardless, you must remain secure in yourself and know that you have the ability to overcome any opinion by the power that you have within yourself.

Don't define your life by other people's view of you. Nor, allow other people's prejudices become a crutch or an excuse. I was once told that "excuses are tools of incompetence that build monuments of nothingness and those that so often use them, rarely accomplish anything". Use hatred and injustice in any area as a catalyst to launch you into your destiny.

The third key is that you have to change you before you change anyone else. Change isn't change until it's changed. Therefore you can't say that you are a different person and you are still doing the "same" things that you have always been doing. Change starts with the person in the mirror. As the Bible says, "you without sin, cast the first stone". In other words, before you begin to critique others, take a hard look at yourself. I had to look closely at my own self and examine what traits were good and what traits were bad. Sometimes it is tough to look in the mirror and say that you may be wrong or the problem is you.

This is a key step in taking off the handcuffs in any area of your life. You have to say that it all begins with me and if I'm not willing to do something different, then I can't expect anyone else to do anything different. If you need to lose weight, you can't judge others for not going to the gym when you refuse to go yourself. If you want to start a business, you can't become envious of other people's success when you refuse to write your own business plan. It all begins with you. You are responsible for the choices you make today to ensure that you have a success and prosperous tomorrow. Are you ready to change and remove those handcuffs?

Questions
1) What are some stereotypes you've heard about other groups? About the group you belong to? Why are those stereotypes ridiculous?
2) Can you think of any excuses why you or others can't overcome those stereotypes? Why are those excuses ridiculous?
3) What are some area in your life that you need to change or have made excuses in?

THE FOURTH KEY: REMEMBER YOUR SAVING GRACES

Nobody's life is pure hell. Nobody's.

I'm not downplaying anyone in any type of unfortunate circumstance. And, I won't deny that some situations are probably so bad, there's no such thing as a cloud with a silver lining. It would be condescending for me to deny these things. What I will say is this: in the darkest moments, when the end of the world seems just moments away, I ask you to please, please, please remember your Saving Graces.

What are the Saving Graces? The things or people in your life that signify a spark of hope, strength and endurance.

They're the reason why when the world seems like it's going to end, you don't end with it.

No matter who you are and what you're going through, you've experienced something good or inspirational at some point. You laughed, smiled or simply felt warmth you may not be able to muster during whatever you're currently going through. Fine. I understand, I've been there.

I'm not asking you to change how you feel, but *remember how you felt*.

I have three Saving Graces that have served me throughout my adult life whenever my struggles seemed to get the best of me. My first Saving Grace is God.

I'm not here to tell you what you should believe, but I don't have a problem telling you what I believe. I believe in God, and I believe He sent His son to die for the sins of mankind. And, when I think about the sacrifice that Jesus made not just for me, but all of humanity, I can easily walk away from the brink of despair.

This book is not a sermon, but it is a true story of what has helped me to become the person that I am today. There have been many times in my life that I have felt frustrated, depressed and even hopeless and I recognize that someone and/or something greater than me had me through those times. You won't see me on the cover of a book proclaiming that I am a "self made …", because God made me into the person that I am and not myself.

One of the major keys of me unlocking my handcuffs has been my dependence on God and trust in Him to know that even when I'm at the end of my rope, there is still more room left on His. To sum up this saving grace, I have included another poem by my father, Larry Alton Manley:

Pray Before The Storm
This is one of those afternoon's
The wind is blowing rapidly
Whistling a wide variety of tunes
Taking over the stage gradually

All kind of thoughts hit your mind;
"I wonder how good I've been".
Wondering if this is the final time
And will I see Bill Cosby again.

It's a trip, the way we trip;
When the ways of the land
Makes us wonder if somehow we've slipped
From letting God command

I wonder if there comes a storm;
Or if the wind blows to hard.
We immediately loose our form,
And call emergency to GOD.

I want you to notice, I said we;
Because we all do the same.
So this poem is for you and me;
We need to believe in GOD's name

I'm rapping about how we should stand;
Believing in good times, as well as bad.
Always trusting and confiding in the man;
In happy times as well as sad.

We often turn only in time of despair;
The FATHER will always be the judge.
Regardless of the situation GOD's always there;
And he never carries any type of grudge.
Larry Alton Manley

My second Saving Grace is my mother, or, more specifically, the strength she's displayed as she struggled to support our family over the years. I would be remiss if I didn't take the opportunity to not only reflect on the wonderful mother that I do have, but to thank her for being the woman that she has always been.

My mother has been a solid rock in my life since the moment of my birth. My mom has been my watchtower to ensure that I made the best decisions that I could possibly make as a young man. I'm not trying to create any type of emotion with these comments, nor am I trying to distance anyone who may have a different relationship with their mother, if any. My intent is to say that someone has been a solid rock to you. It may have been your grandmother, the football coach, or the leader of the Boys/Girls club in your neighborhood. These individuals laid the core foundation of who you are today.

Without my mom, I'm not sure where I would be. Locked up? Six feet under? Who knows? What I do know is that she has had a tremendous impact on my life and because of my love and respect for her, I had a reason to not sell drugs, hang out on the corner or to get someone pregnant. No, I'm not saying I'm perfect, because I am not; I am saying that my mom served as my saving grace to help me make better choices.

My third Saving Grace is, oddly, not something I consider very positive, but it has been a beacon that helped me find my way when things seemed dark. My third Saving Grace comes from my father. His words to me, from that day at the jail so long ago, "Don't end up like me."

I carry these words as a spiritual tattoo on my life. "Don't end up like me." To you, that phrase could be, "you are just like your father", "you will never amount to anything", or "you can't do that". Whatever the statement, you must use it as a stepping stone and not a stumbling block. These phrases can ultimately place "mental handcuffs" on your life but you have to use them for your good. Let the world know that you are captain of your fate and not someone's statement that may have been said out of hurt and resentment. I had to come to a point in my life where I could be different or get lost in the crowd.

I didn't want people to ask how was Alton doing and get the response 'locked up' or 'running the streets'. I was bigger than that and you are bigger than that. You have to realize that you are bigger and better than your environment and you can't allow people's words to handcuff your future.

Do you want to be different? Do you want to leave a positive legacy and change your family tree? Do you want your name to be a sweet memory when people think about you? Then get up and do something different, stop making excuses and fight until you have what you want out of life!

Questions
1) What are your saving graces? Take a moment to reflect on how those saving graces have guided you throughout your life.
2) When people think of you, what comes to mind or what do they say to describe you? Do their words match who you are?
3) What type of lasting legacy do you want to leave? If there was one thing you could change in your family tree, what would it be?

THE FIFTH KEY:
TAKE OFF THE HANDCUFFS

Believe it or not, unlocking the handcuffs that bind you is only half the process. You still need to take them off if you have any hopes of freeing yourself from the incarceration so many of us suffer through our entire lives. Physically, this would be a simple thing . . . take the keys I've given you, undo the clasp, and let the metal loops fall to the floor. Easy, right?

Matters of the mind are rarely that simple.

A short book can never give you all the tools you need to reach a goal, beat an addiction, overcome a disability, or move past abuse. It can't make you love yourself, make you love others, or make you let yourself be loved. It can't heal sickness, it can extinguish grief, and it can't make you happy. It can't take off the handcuffs for you.

What's really holding you back? What is the basis of your incarceration?

9 out of 10 people, when confronted with that question, will say the answer is fear.

The thing is, if this were a test, I couldn't give you full credit for that one. Fear can mean so many things, too much in fact.

Is it a fear of failure or a fear of success and all its responsibilities?

Is it a fear of falling in love or a fear of breaking a heart?

What are you afraid of?

Make a list of your most secret fears. It's alright, the list is just for you. Take this as an opportunity to be honest with yourself.

After speaking to thousands of people across the country, I realized that many people don't know how to be released from the "mental handcuffs" on their life. I can stand on a stage and speak my heart out, but sometimes that is not enough. That is why I decided to write this book because I wanted people to wrap their hands around a solution and feel like they can make it.

Even with the book, I wanted people to be able to physically write out their challenges, goals, and identify areas in their lives in which they still have on "mental handcuffs." To compliment the book, I created the No More Handcuffs Companion guide that allows you to work through the barriers preventing you from succeeding in any area and help you to establish tangible and attainable goals that will help you achieve your dreams. This guide is only for those individuals who are serious about removing the mental handcuffs from their lives. I want to challenge people to go higher in their life, regardless of their current situation.

People say I'm too old, or I don't have enough money, or I don't have time; but remember, change begins with you. Ghandi said it best, "become the change you want to see in the world." In the No More Handcuffs Companion Guide, one of the things that I share are the keys to releasing your handcuffs and expound on each one in detail. I will briefly share 7 of the 14 keys below in the form of the acronym R.E.L.E.A.S.E:

1) R: Realize that you mind is going to do one of two things, it is going to create a prison or a palace. You have to decide everyday about the choices that you make.

2) E: Education is the key. In line with the United Negro College Fund saying, a mind is truly a terrible thing to waste. You must constantly learn more, not only in academia, but in your area of expertise or passion. I have to constantly learn more about professional speaking and training as well as being an author to continue to excel.

3) L: You must love yourself enough to know where you are now is not your final destination. You must realize that if you can see yourself in a better place, then the only person stopping you from getting there is you. Realize that if you can imagine it, you can obtain it.

4) E: You must raise your expectation if you want to take off the cuffs and obtain a better life. If you want more, you have to expect more. You can't live a life of low expectations and believe that you will obtain greatness. You must raise your expectations if you want to raise your standard of living.

5) A: What you focus on is what you will attract. You have to realize that the Law of Attraction is critical to your success. You must focus on removing those handcuffs and succeeding in life so that everything that you will attract will lead to that very thing.

6) S: You must continually work on self development. I tell students, that sometimes you have to turn off the Playstation and Xbox and read a book or do your homework. In other words, you are your greatest asset so you have to take time developing yourself.

7) E: You must find examples and mentors that will help you make it to the next level and help to remove those "mental handcuffs" on your life. I have some select mentors that have guided me in certain areas of my life and if it wasn't for their leadership, I would not be the person that I am today.

The choice is yours, are you ready to take off those handcuffs?

Questions

1) What would you do if you weren't afraid?
2) Where would your life be if you didn't leave in fear?
3) From 1-10, with 10 being the strongest and 1 the weakest, how bad do you want to take off your mental handcuffs? Ok, now do something about it!

CONCLUSION

No More Handcuffs means everything, physically, mentally, emotionally, and even spiritually, that has held you back is now released. No More Handcuffs is a declaration that your past no longer has a hold on you and now you can capture your dream and walk into your destiny. For years, I have always wondered, "why was I here" or "what is my place in this world". Now I realized as an empowerment expert and success coach, that my place is to help other people realize their full potential and to help them remove the "mental handcuffs" off of their lives. As I was sharing with one of my coaching clients, "once you identify your "why", the "how" becomes irrelevant". In other words, the moment you identify that you are here for something greater, then how it will happen is no longer an issue. Why, because you now have the passion to fuel your tank while you reach to obtain your goals and dreams.

I want you to view this book as the key to your ignition to get you going in the right direction. You are more than a winner, so why quit the game? Stay focused and realize that if you have the passion and the desire to remove those handcuffs, then nothing will be withheld from you. I have sprinkled my father's words throughout the book, but now I close with my own words:

No More Handcuffs
Forgetting things that are behind
Forgetting my past and pressing toward tomorrow
Forgetting yesterday and renewing my mind
Forgetting my mistakes and erasing all of my sorrow
No More Handcuffs
Focusing on a new beginning and new lease on life
Focusing on the present and everything in front of me
Focusing on the promise of a brighter day without strife
Focusing on my future and knowing that I am finally free
No More Handcuffs
Fighting to remove all the chains that have been holding me
down
Fighting to reach a destiny that I thought I had lost
Fighting to be released of every barrier pulling me to the ground
Fighting to capture my dream and let my past know that Now,
I AM THE BOSS
No More Handcuffs
Freedom is now in view
Freedom is now mine and bondage has left my domain
Freedom, oh freedom, how fresh and anew
Freedom, it can truly ring, deep from within my veins
NO MORE HANDCUFFS by Alton Jamison